The Adventures of Bixie & Myron

Dedicated to the memory of my mothe

Marie Hurda Kneitinger

April 1st 1931 - June 29th 2020

Children's books series by

Robert Knietinger

Myron the mouse comes in the apartment through a hole in the wall and his feet are dirty. Bixie asks, "Is that you Myron!?"
Myron says, "Yes " and Bixie says "Come on out, Robert is not home."

Myron starts running around and starts to get the rug all diry. Bixie sees this and is starting to panic. She doesn't know what to do! The rug is dirty and Bixie worries because she knows that her owner Robert will be coming home soon. Bixie doesn't know what to do to save Myron from Robert's punishment for making the rug dirty.

Bixie says, "Myron, I'm trying to save you from Robert. I'm trying to save

your life! I know you're trying to be friends but you're getting into a lot of trouble with Robert."

Myron keeps running around and breaks something that Robert really likes. So Bixie starts to panic even more. Robert will see it when he gets home. Robert will think that Bixie broke the item.

Myron says, "I am really sorry that I am getting into so much trouble. I will try to be better."
"I know I caused a lot of trouble for you and you are trying to take the blame for me."

Myron often comes out when Robert is not home. Bixie knows that Robert will try to get rid of his friend Myron. To make Myron hide, Bixie tries to chase Myron back into the hole in the wall so he is safe.

Bixie says to Myron, "I want you to go back into your home where you will be safe."

Robert comes home and opens the door. He sees Myron the mouse and tries to catch him.

Bixie says to Myron, "Get back into your hole before Robert catches you!"

Myron feels bad for Bixie because Robert will think that he made the mess, so Myron brings a big piece of cheese to make Bixie feel better.

Myron tells Bixie, "I feel so bad that you are taking the punishment for me."

keep on movin
I AM SO ANGRY LOOK At tHiS BRO ken GLASS on the FLOOR
Bixie HeReis A piece oFFeRinG I Am SO SORRY

Bixie is happy to see that Myron made it back to the hole in the wall where he lives. For now he is safe.

Bixie thanks Myron for helping him to be safe.

At night, when Robert is sleeping, Myron will come out to play with Bixie. This time, however, Robert sees the mouse and grabs a broom to swat him. Myron knows that he shouldn't have come out.

When Robert leaves for work the next day, Bixie sees Myron and tells him to stay home in his hole in the wall. Nothing can happen to Myron if he is in his hole when Robert comes home.

Myron says, "Thanks for telling me to stay in my home. I feel safe here."

Myron is so scared of Robert that Myron will not come out. Myron won't come out at all now.

Bixie says Myron, "I know that you are scared of Robert. I wish that you were not scared of him so you would come out and play when he is not home."

Myron says, "But every time I come out I break something. I love to run around so much!"

Bixie tells Myron that Robert is not home so Myron is safe to come out and play.

Bixie says, "Don't be stubborn Myron. I'll give you a piece of cheese if you come out and play."

Myron is happy to be able to come out when Robert isn't home, he has not played with Bixie in a long time.

Myron and Bixie are having fun with each other. Then Bixie hears Robert come home early. Bixie tells Myron to run to his home before Robert sees him.

Bixie says, "I am having so much fun with you Myron when Robert isn't home."

Bixie is also excited to see Robert home. Bixie is excited to get so much attention from Robert, he feeds and pets her.

Myron comes to see Bixie getting so much attention. Myron feels sad that he can't come out and get some loving attention too, but he knows it is not safe.

Bixie feels so bad to be in the middle between Robert and Myron. Bixie and Myron are good friends but Robert doesn't like mice.

Bixie says, "I wish that I wasn't in the middle. I feel so bad for you Myron."

Myron says, "It's tough being in the middle. I know you are taking the blame for my mischief."

Bixie doesn't want to see anything bad happen to Myron, he is so worried that Robert will catch Myron. Every time Myron comes out Bixie panics if Robert is home at the time.

Bixi says, "I am worried about you Myron. I don't want to see anything bad happen to you."

Bixie wishes Robert would become friends with Myron so all three of them would become good friends together. If they became friends she would not need to be worried all the time.

Myron comes out and starts running around again when Robert isn't home. He breaks something that Robert really likes, Robert's favorite NFL bottle. Bixie worries that Robert will see it when he comes home and thinks that Bixie broke it..

Robert came home early and saw the broken bottle. He shouted, "What happened to my favorite NFL bottle?!"

Bixie replies, "I'm sorry, I broke. It was an accident."

Robert, "I'm so angry with you right now!"

Meanwhile, Myron is watching all of this from inside his hole.

Myron feels ashamed about what he has done. His best friend Bixie is going to get in big trouble. He wonders what he can do to make it right.

Myron says, "I am sorry about all the trouble I caused. I feel so bad for you Bixie."

Myron rushes out of his hole. Hoping that Robert won't swat him, Myron says, "I'm the one that did it, I broke your bottle. Don't blame Bixie."

Dropping a big hunk of cheddar he found in the garbage, Myron states, "I bring you this piece of cheese as a peace offering."

Robert chased Myron around the apartment with a broom, knocking over all sorts of stuff. Myron finally escaped back into his hole. Even though Robert did not accept his peace offering, Myron was happy knowing Bixie is off the hook.

THE END

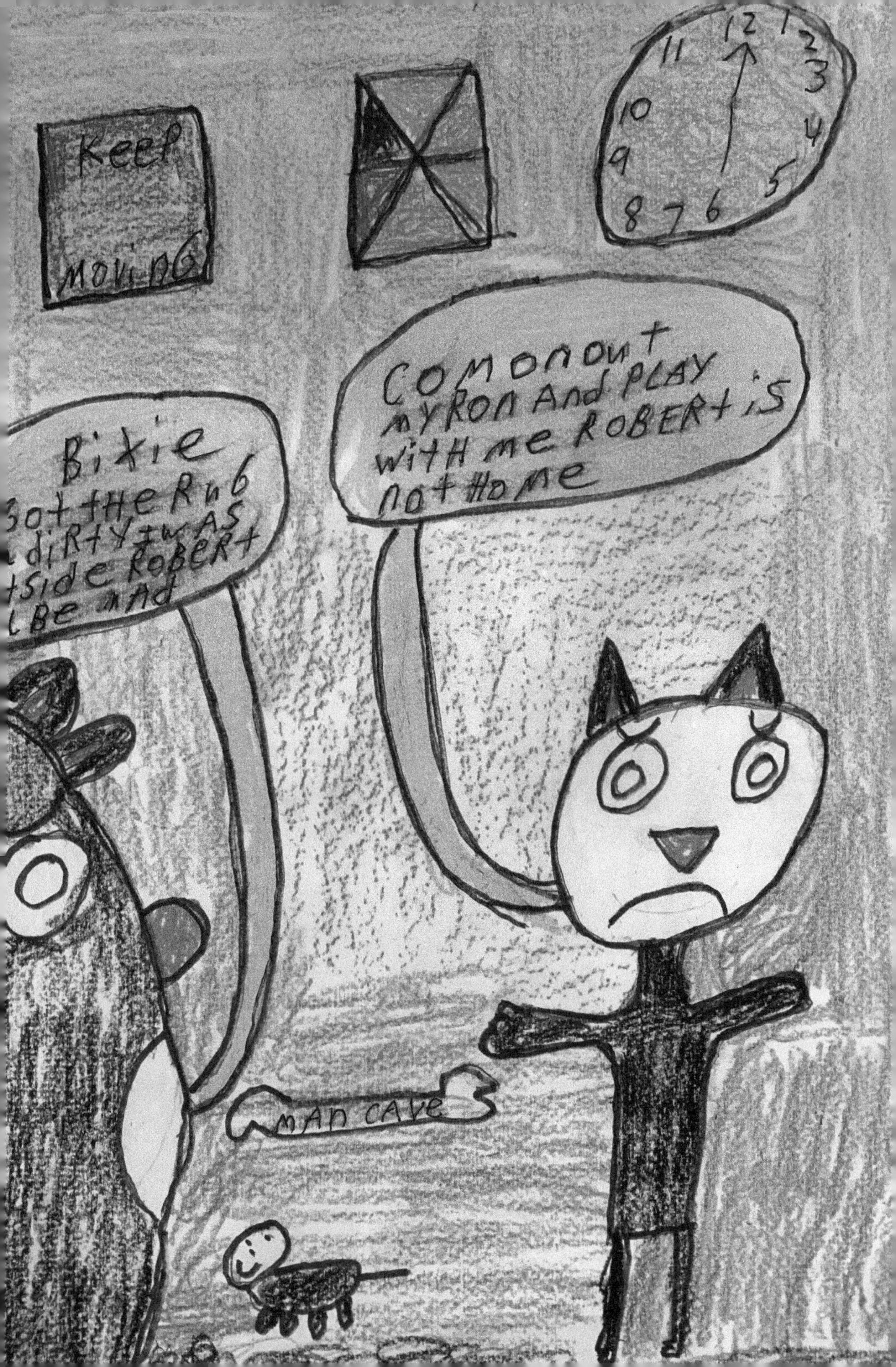

CPSIA information can be obtained
at www.ICGtesting.com
Printed in the USA
BVHW022141250421
605816BV00032B/2163